I Still Love You, Dad

This title has been published with the co-operation of Cherrytree Books
Amicus Illustrated is published by Amicus
P.O. Box 1329, Mankato, Minnesota 56002

Printed in Mankato, Minnesota, USA by CG Book Printers, a division of
Corporate Graphics

Library of Congress Cataloging-in-Publication Data

Bode, Ann de.
 I still love you, Dad / Ann de Bode.
     p. cm. -- (Side by side)
 Summary: Laura wishes very much that her father still lived at home, so when
her mother brings a man home for a visit Laura misbehaves in hopes of driving
him off, but then finds herself liking him.
 ISBN 978-1-60753-177-7 (library binding)
 [1. Divorce--Fiction. 2. Behavior--Fiction. 3. Family life--Fiction.] I. Title.
 PZ7.B633618Ias 2012
 [E]--dc22
                                    2011002239

13-digit ISBN: 978-1-60753-177-7 First Edition 1110987654321
This edition © Evans Brothers Limited 2011
2A Portman Mansions, Chiltern Street, London W1U 6NR, United Kingdom

© Van In, Lier, 1995. Van In Publishers, Grote Markt 39, 2500 Lier, Belgium
Originally published in Belgium as Maar jij blijft mijn papa

Today is the school play!
Everyone is chatting and getting ready.
But Laura doesn't feel like joining in.

"What's the matter, Laura?" asks Tim.
"No one's coming to watch
me," says Laura, crying.

Laura's dad has moved.
Her mom and dad don't love
each other any more. Laura
lives with her mom and her
brother Thomas.

Laura misses her dad.
And she has to do more
jobs to help her mom.

When Laura stays with Dad, he gives her lots of presents. Laura doesn't want presents. She wants Dad to come back home.

"I know just how you feel,"
says Tim. His parents don't
live together either.
Laura starts to cheer up, and
gets ready for the play.

Now it's Tim's turn to look unhappy.
"You're thinking about your mom and dad
now, aren't you?" says Laura.
"Yes."

The play is about to start. Laura
peeps through the curtains on stage.
Look — it's Mom!

And there's Dad, too.
Laura points to an empty
seat — next to Mom.
Perhaps they'll make up!
she thinks.

Laura is the star of the show.
She feels brave because she knows
Mom and Dad are watching.

Afterward Mom says, "You were wonderful!"
But where's Dad?
"He had to go," says Mom.
Laura's happy feeling starts to disappear.

Back at home, Mom tells the children
to get ready for a visitor.
"Who's coming?" asks Laura angrily.
"A new friend of mine," says Mom. "A man."

14

Laura doesn't want a man to come over.
What will she say to him?
What if he's ugly or bald?
Or has a huge nose?

Thomas just says, "Don't worry. It's nice
that Mom's got a new friend."
"But what about Dad?" asks Laura.
"He's still our dad," says Thomas.

16

Laura is mad and fed up.
"I know!" she thinks. "I'll be so naughty
that this man won't want to be Mom's
friend any more!"

Laura starts her plan right away.
"Take your feet off the table," says Mom.
"OK," says Laura, and takes off her shoes.
"Well you only said take my feet off," she says.

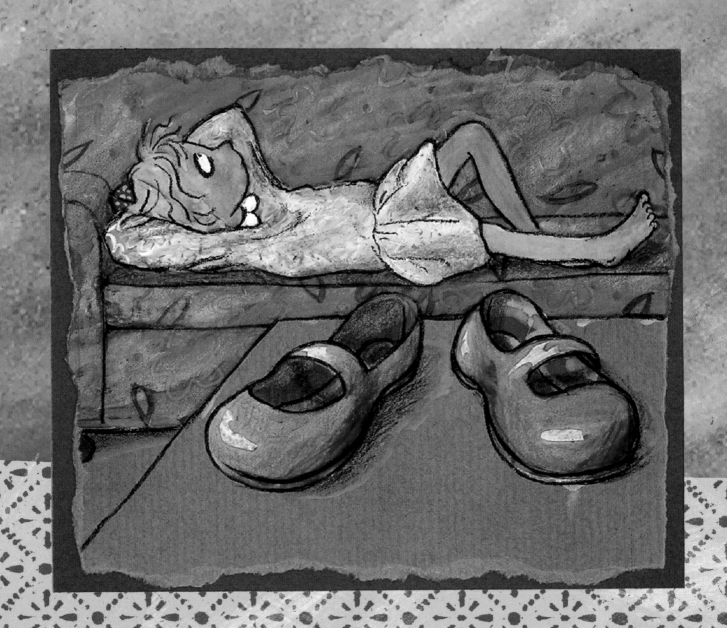

"Why do we have to have the fancy tablecloth?" she asks rudely, and picks her nose. "Stop that," says Mom.

The visitor arrives.

"Laura, this is John," says Mom.

Laura is surprised. He looks quite normal.

But she still doesn't like him.

When Mom goes out to the kitchen,
Laura pulls a silly face at John.
John just laughs and winks at her.

John looks at the books in the bookcase.
"We had lots more books when Dad
lived here," says Laura.
"You must miss him," says John.

"The table looks very neat," says John.
"We always have it like this," replies Laura.
"Quite right — fit for a little
princess like you."

Slurp, slurp! Laura eats her soup noisily.
"Eat nicely," grumbles Mom.
Laura takes no notice.

John is sitting in Dad's place.
"He shouldn't be there," thinks Laura.
But deep down she likes John.
She feels very confused. What about Dad?

Laura accidentally drops her cup.
"Oh no!" she thinks. Everything's gone
wrong since Mom and Dad split up.
Even her plot against John hasn't worked.

"Would you like any more?" asks Mom.
"No thanks," says John. "I'm full."
"Huh! Dad could eat much more than you!
He'd have at least four helpings of
everything!" says Laura.

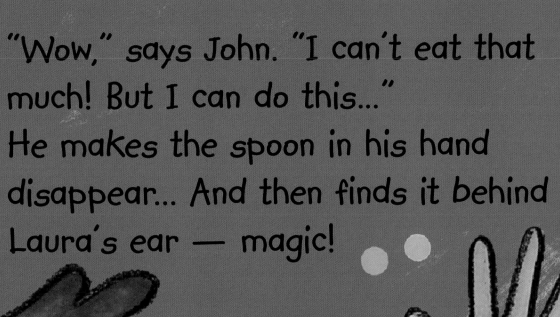

"Wow," says John. "I can't eat that much! But I can do this..."
He makes the spoon in his hand disappear... And then finds it behind Laura's ear — magic!

"Oh no — look at the time!" thinks Laura.
Her dad is about to pick her up.
He mustn't see John!
She runs to find her bag.
"Is there a fire?" asks Mom.

The doorbell rings. It's Dad.

"Bye Mom," says Laura.

"Say goodbye to John too," says Mom.

"Goodbye John. Er... see you soon."

And funnily enough, she hopes she will.

Laura doesn't know if she should
tell Dad about John.
But he asks her why she's so quiet.
"Mom had a visitor for supper — a man."

Dad smiles and keeps on driving.
"That's good. Is he nice?" he asks.
"Umm... yes," Laura says. "But you'll
always be my dad."